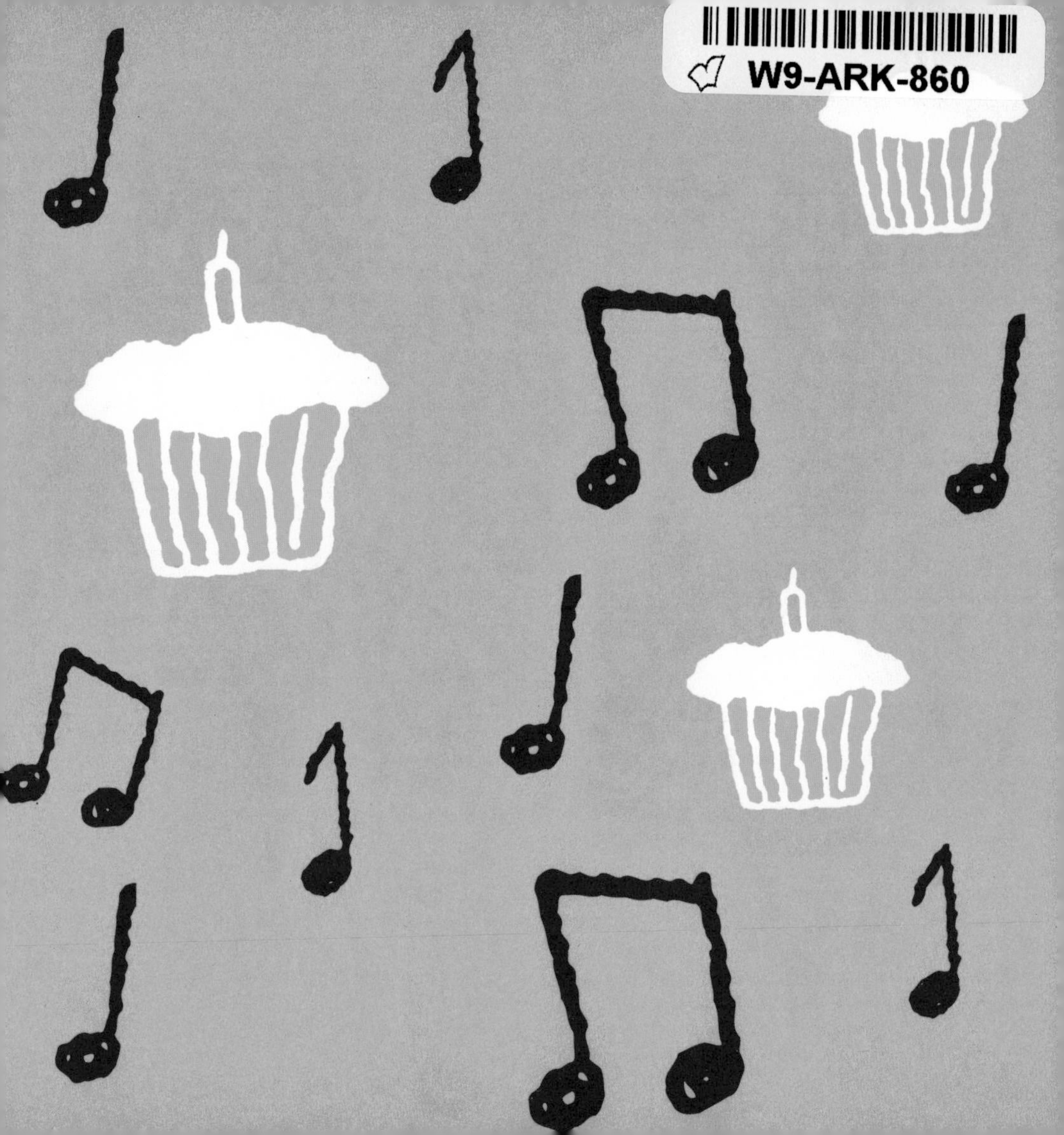

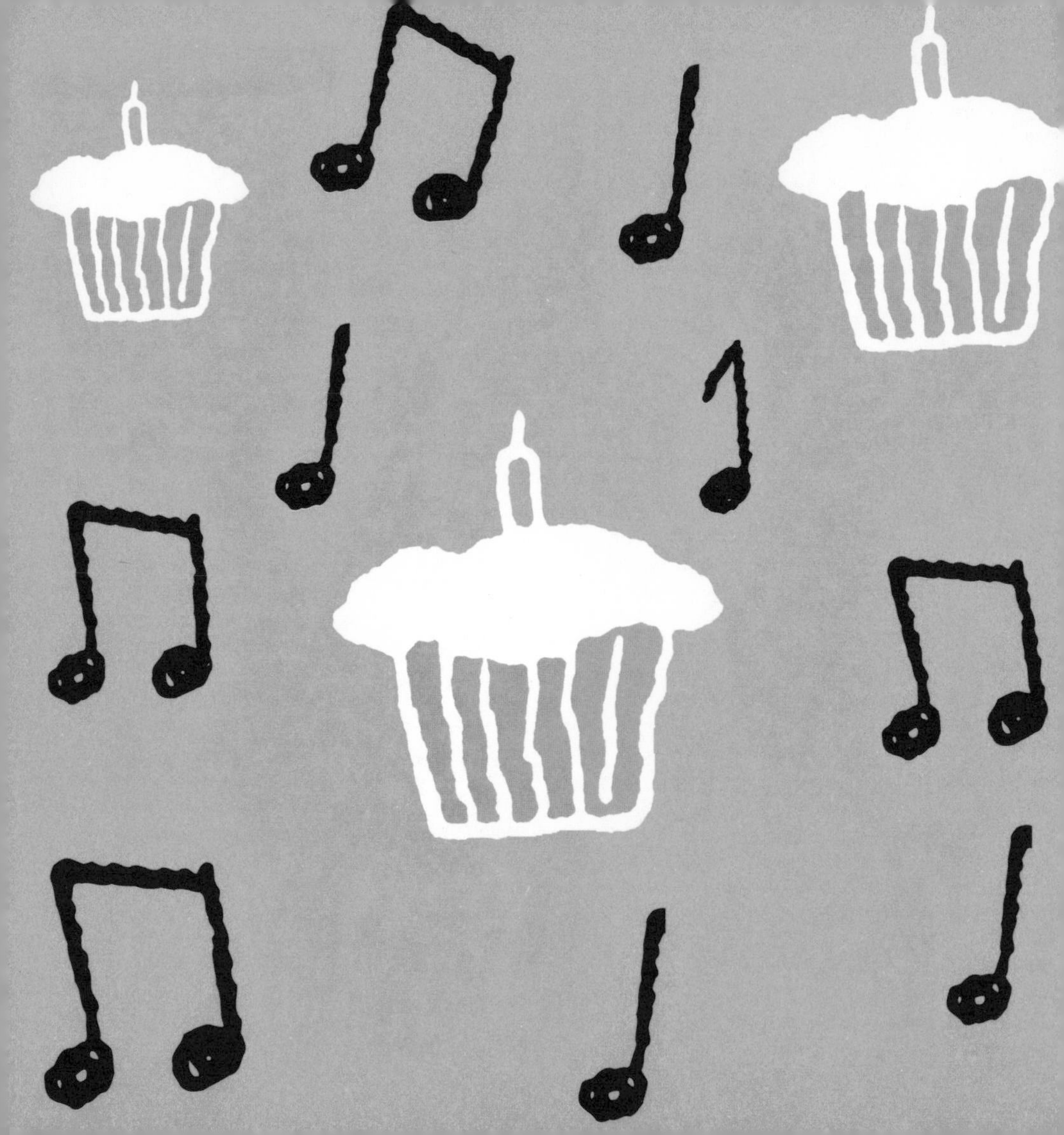

Happy Birthday!
(And One To Glow On)

by
SCHULZ

CollinsPublishersSanFrancisco
A Division of HarperCollins*Publishers*

A Birthday That Takes The Cake

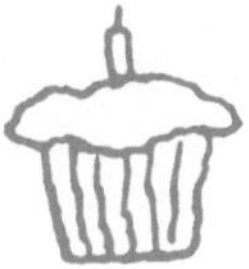

SMAK!

SMAK!

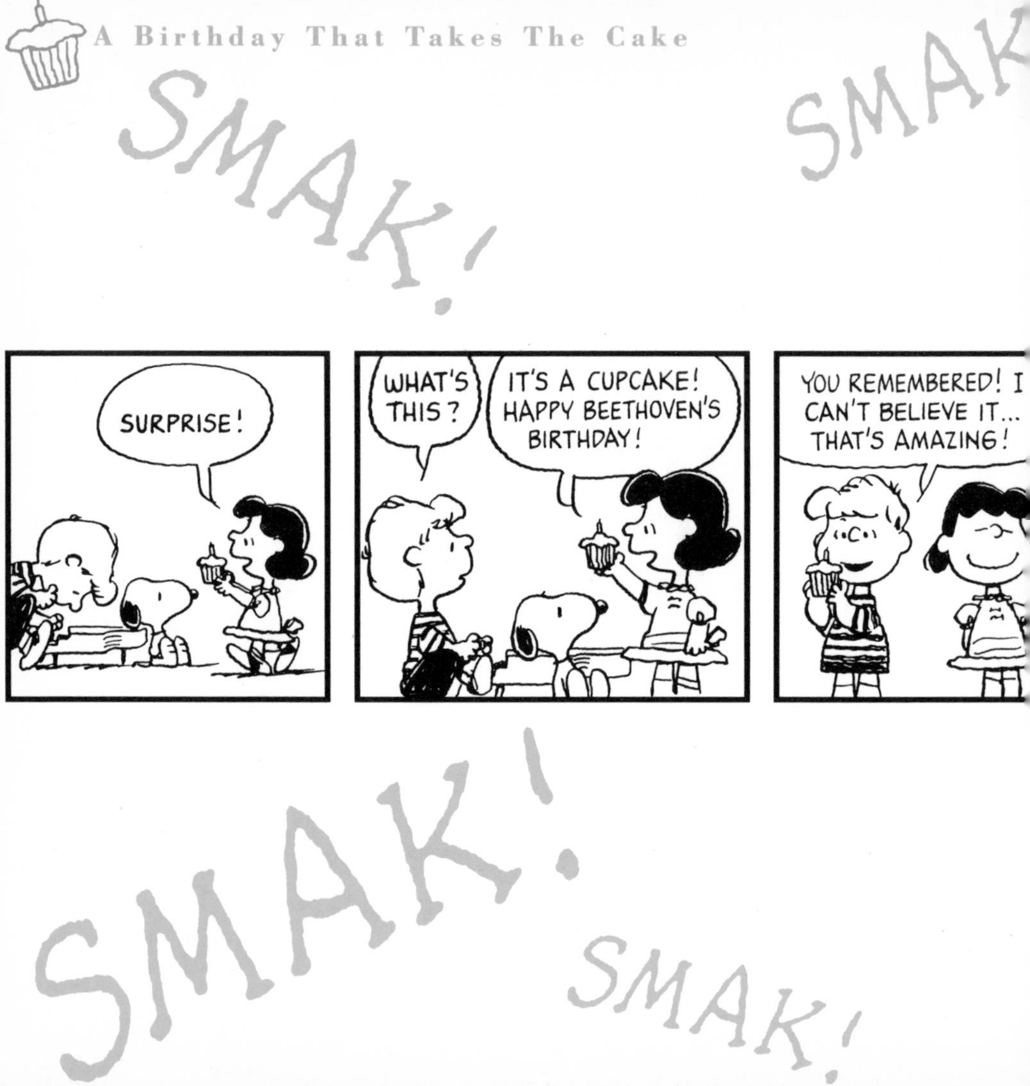
SURPRISE!
WHAT'S THIS?
IT'S A CUPCAKE! HAPPY BEETHOVEN'S BIRTHDAY!
YOU REMEMBERED! I CAN'T BELIEVE IT... THAT'S AMAZING!

SMAK!

SMAK!

SMAK!

SMAK!

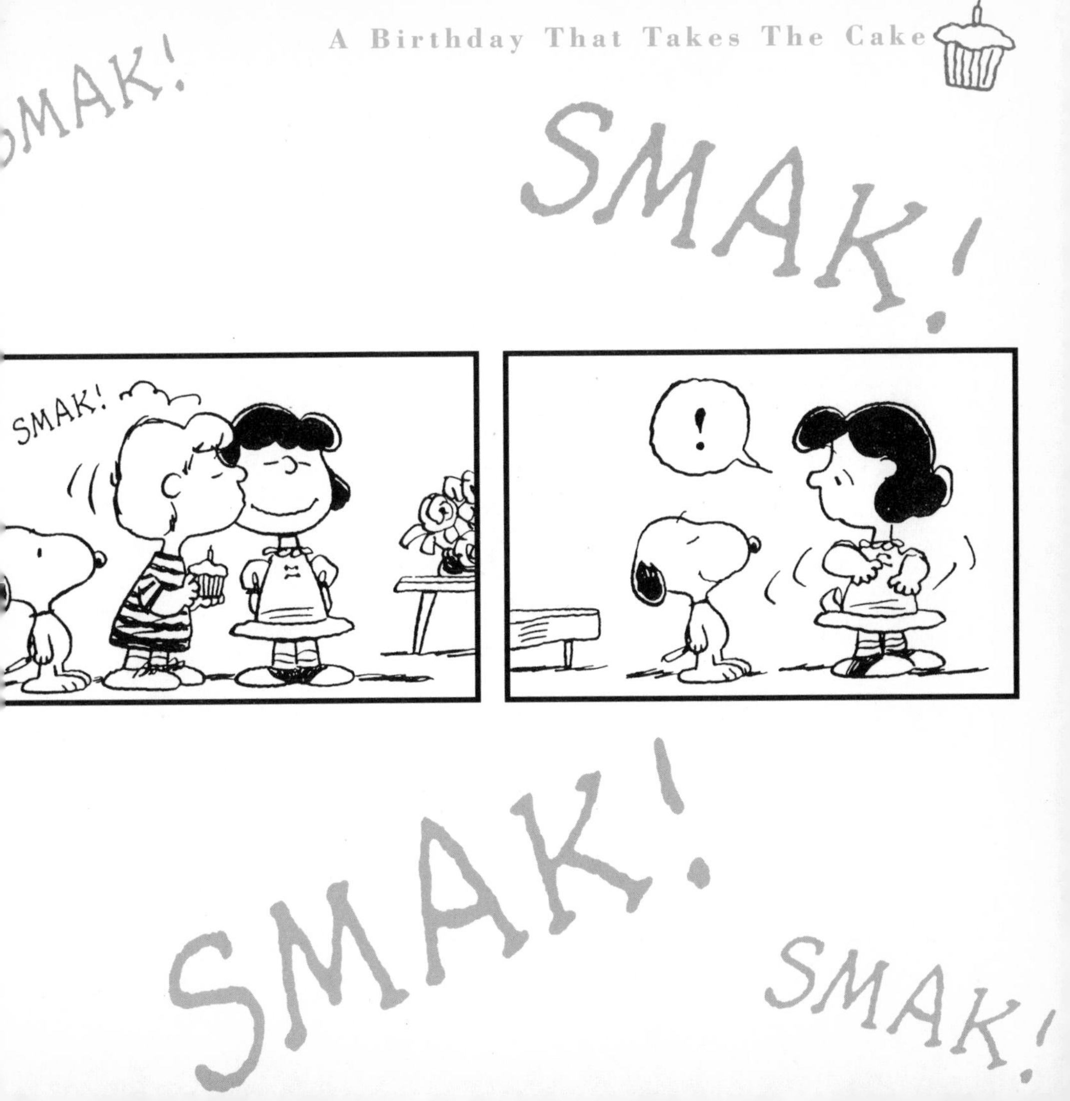
SMAK!
!

SMAK!

SMAK!

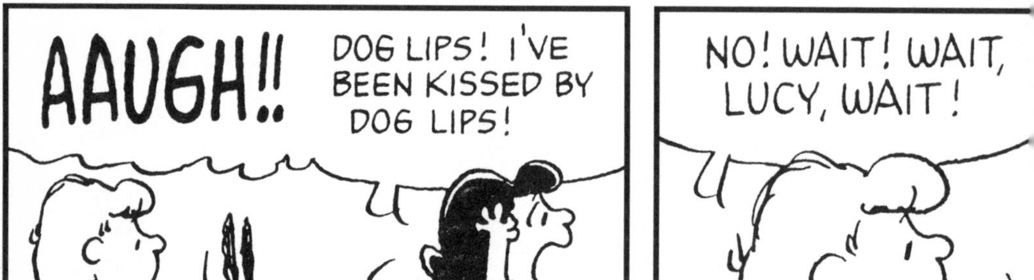
AAUGH!!
DOG LIPS! I'VE BEEN KISSED BY DOG LIPS!
NO! WAIT! WAIT, WAIT, LUCY, WAIT!

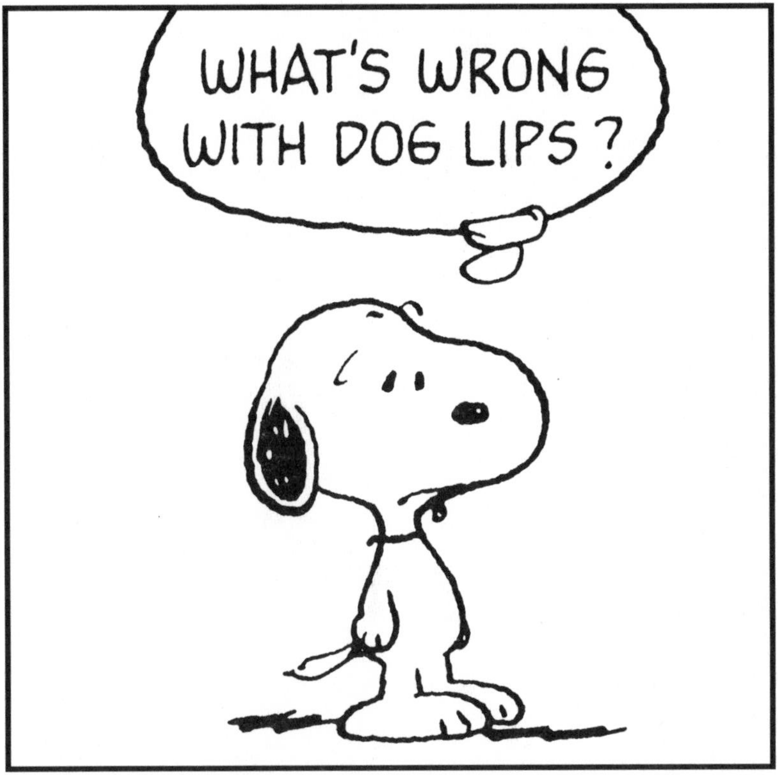
WHAT'S WRONG WITH DOG LIPS?

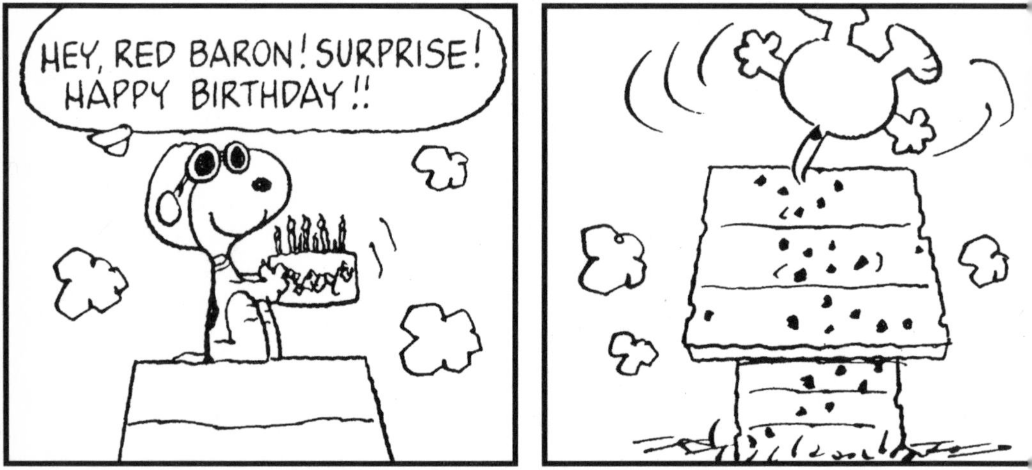
HEY, RED BARON! SURPRISE! HAPPY BIRTHDAY!!

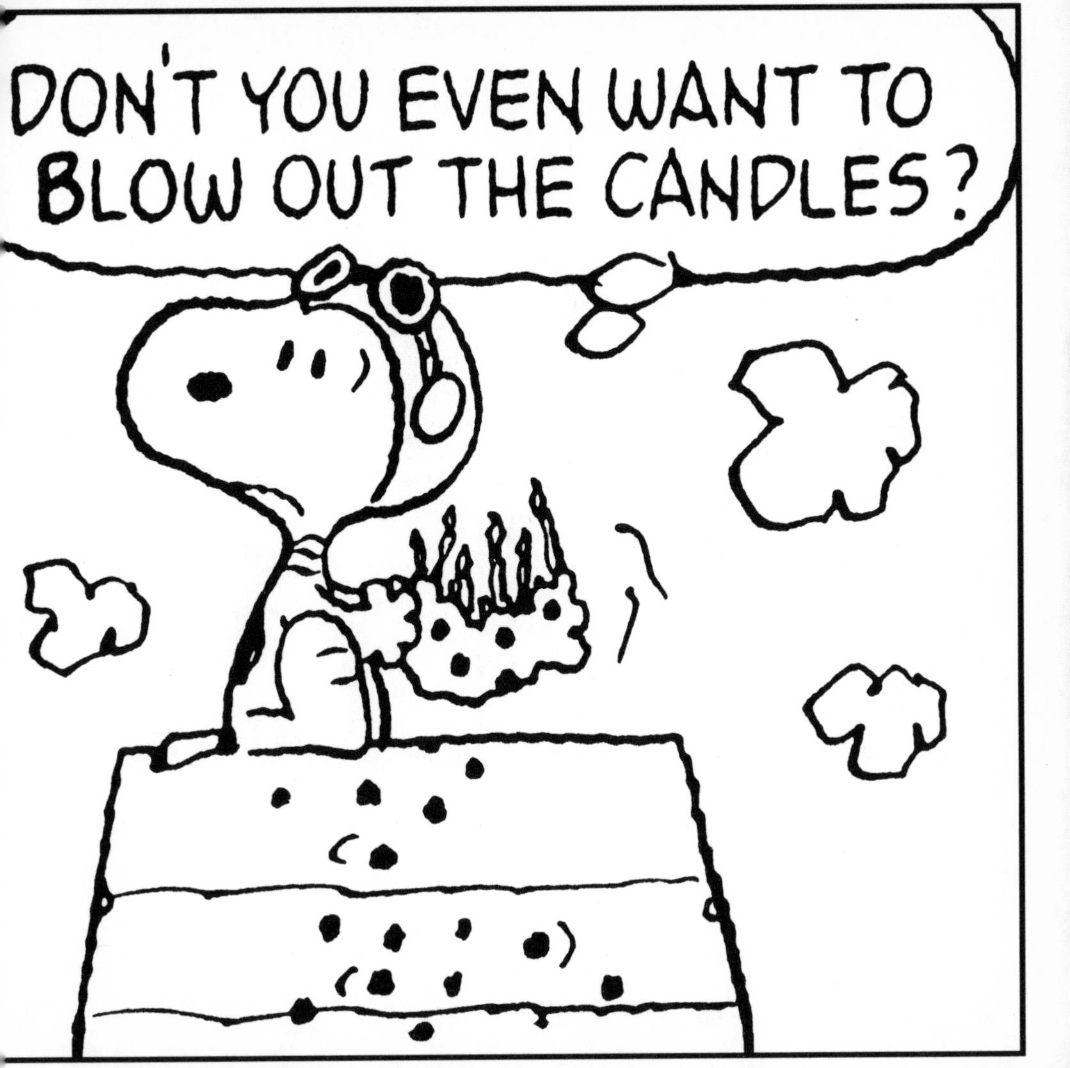
DON'T YOU EVEN WANT TO BLOW OUT THE CANDLES?

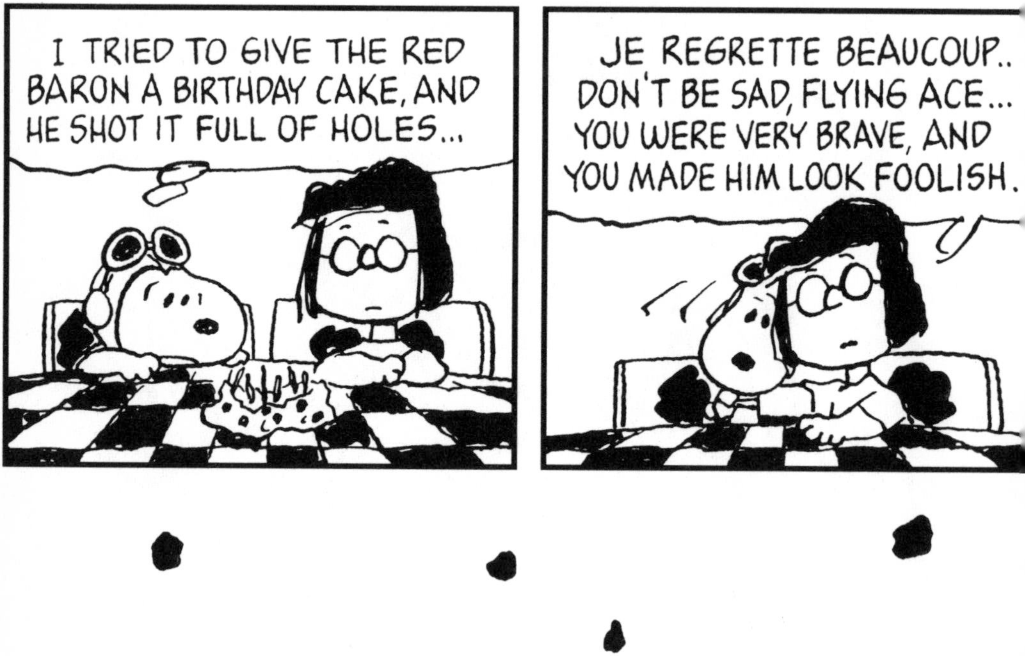
I TRIED TO GIVE THE RED BARON A BIRTHDAY CAKE, AND HE SHOT IT FULL OF HOLES...
JE REGRETTE BEAUCOUP..
DON'T BE SAD, FLYING ACE... YOU WERE VERY BRAVE, AND YOU MADE HIM LOOK FOOLISH.

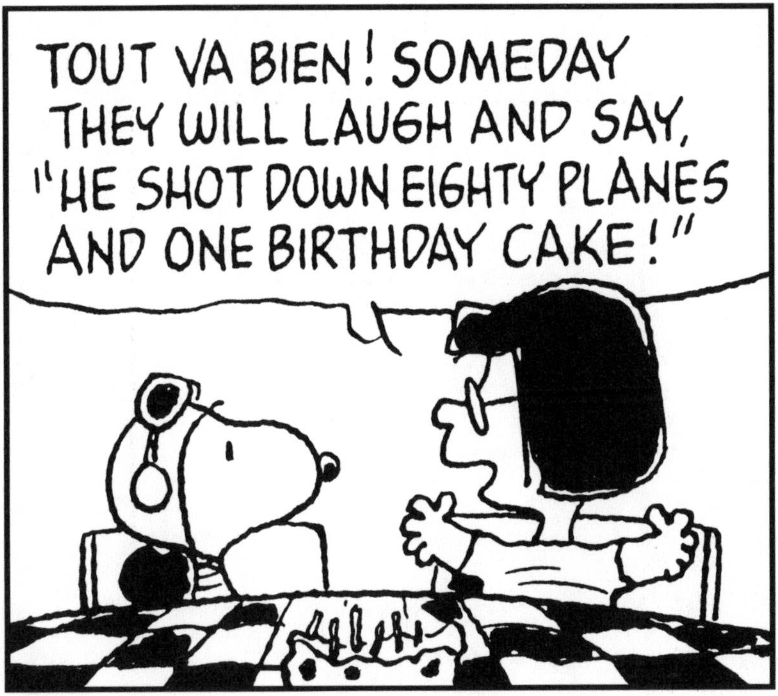
TOUT VA BIEN! SOMEDAY THEY WILL LAUGH AND SAY, "HE SHOT DOWN EIGHTY PLANES AND ONE BIRTHDAY CAKE!"

Birthday Wishes To Glow On

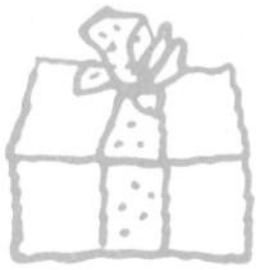

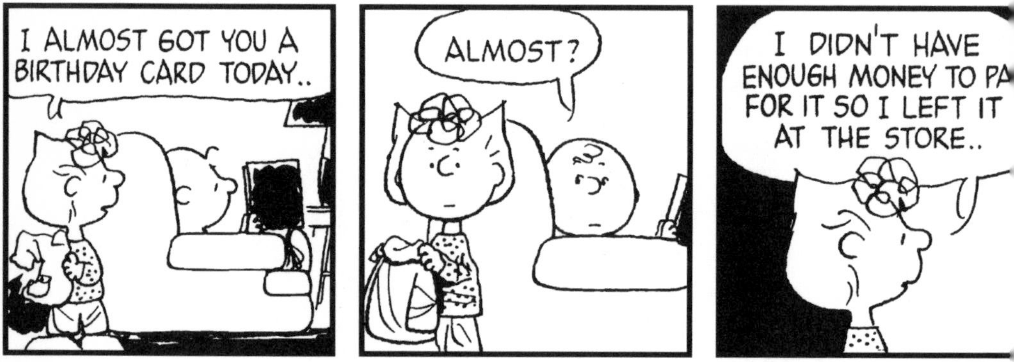
I ALMOST GOT YOU A BIRTHDAY CARD TODAY..
ALMOST?
I DIDN'T HAVE ENOUGH MONEY TO PA
FOR IT SO I LEFT IT AT THE STORE..

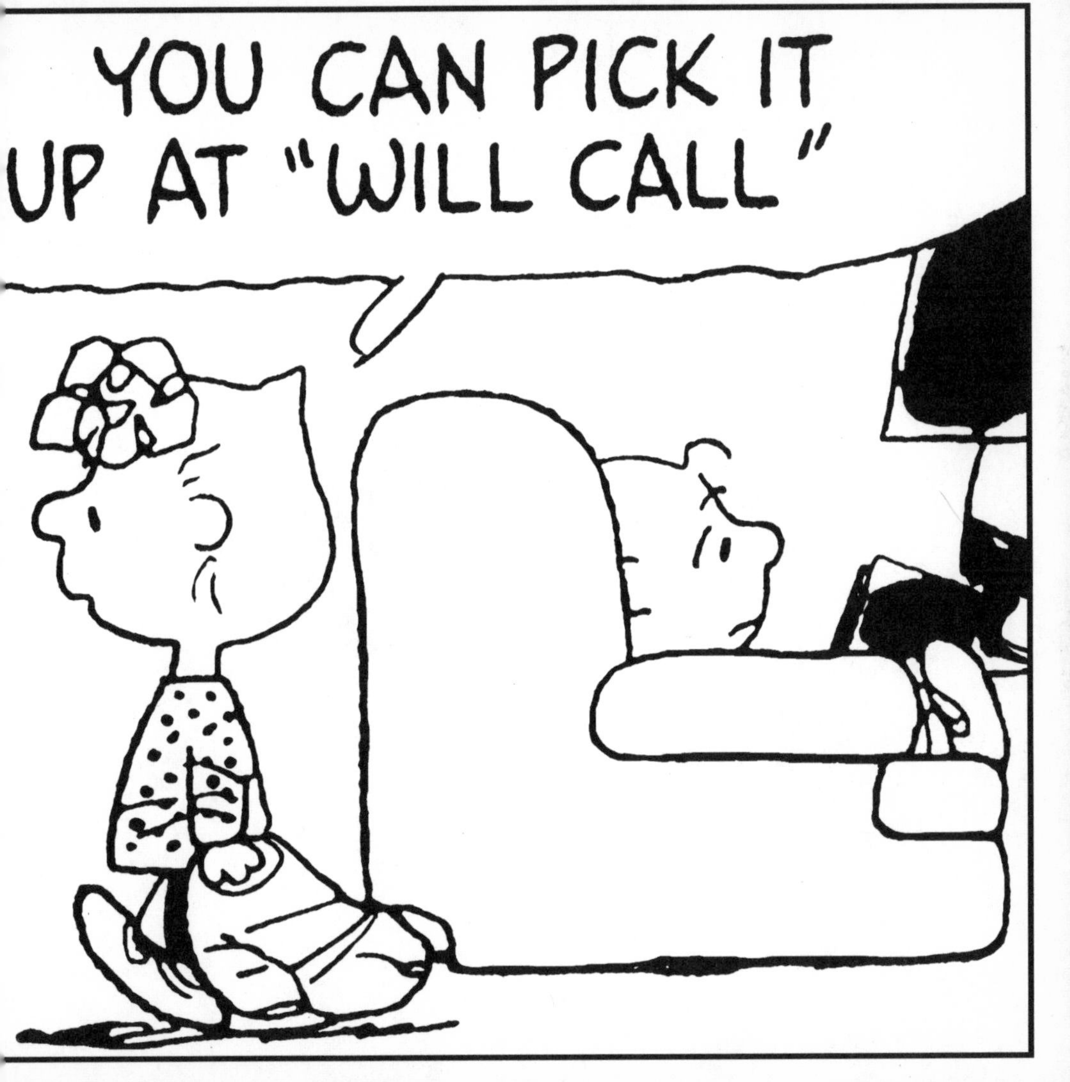
YOU CAN PICK IT UP AT "WILL CALL"

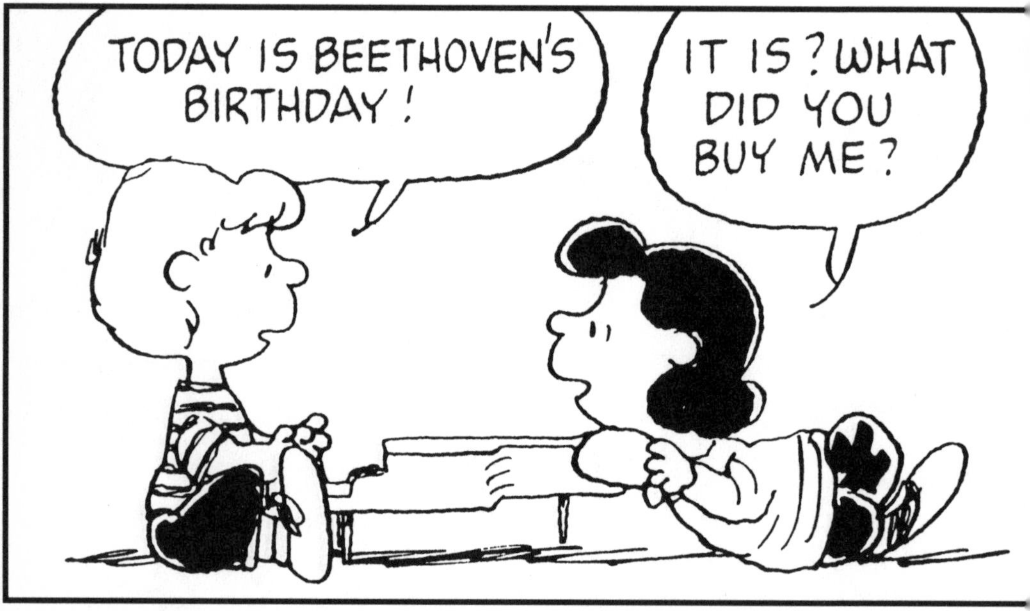
TODAY IS BEETHOVEN'S BIRTHDAY!
IT IS? WHAT DID YOU BUY ME?

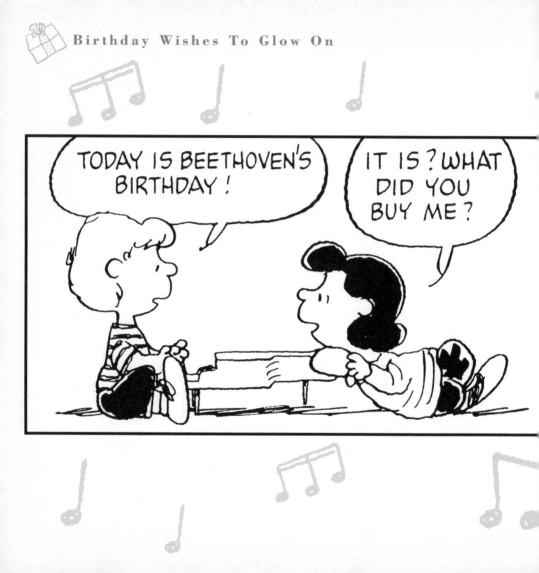

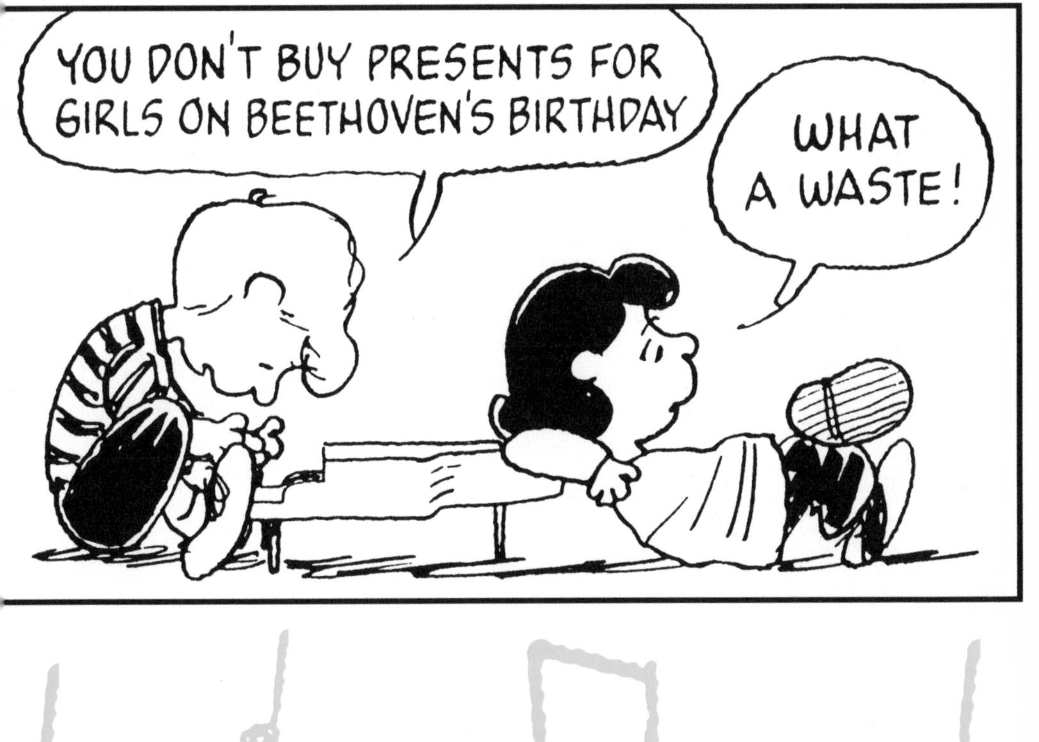
YOU DON'T BUY PRESENTS FOR GIRLS ON BEETHOVEN'S BIRTHDAY
WHAT A WASTE!

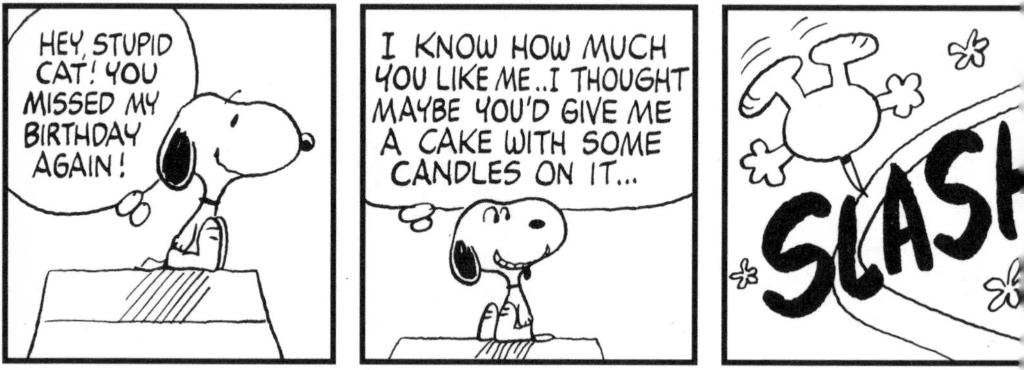
HEY, STUPID CAT! YOU MISSED MY BIRTHDAY AGAIN!
I KNOW HOW MUCH YOU LIKE ME..I THOUGHT MAYBE YOU'D GIVE ME A CAKE WITH SOME CANDLES ON IT...

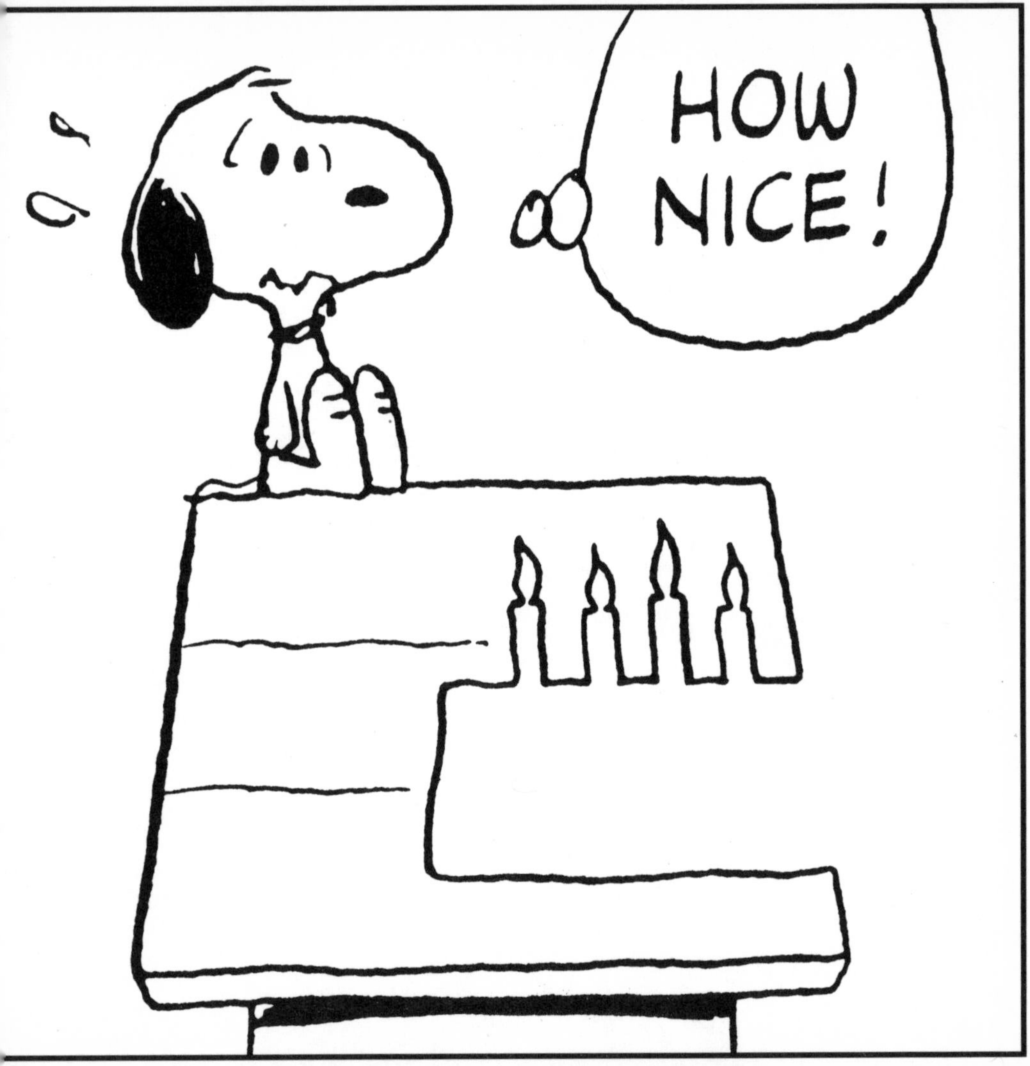
HOW NICE!

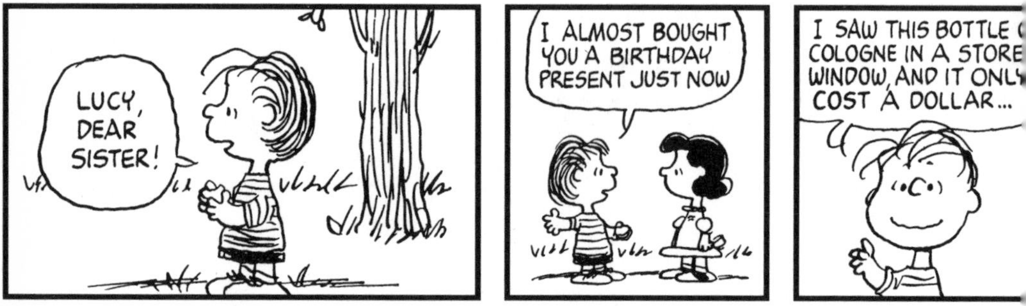
LUCY, DEAR SISTER!
I ALMOST BOUGHT YOU A BIRTHDAY PRESENT JUST NOW
I SAW THIS BOTTLE
COLOGNE IN A STORE
WINDOW, AND IT ONL
COST A DOLLAR...

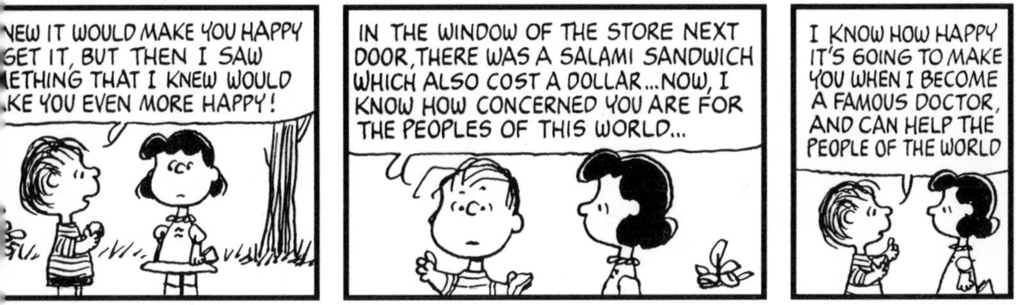
NEW IT WOULD MAKE YOU HAPPY GET IT, BUT THEN I SAW ETHING THAT I KNEW WOULD KE YOU EVEN MORE HAPPY!
IN THE WINDOW OF THE STORE NEXT DOOR, THERE WAS A SALAMI SANDWICH WHICH ALSO COST A DOLLAR...NOW, I KNOW HOW CONCERNED YOU ARE FOR THE PEOPLES OF THIS WORLD...
I KNOW HOW HAPPY IT'S GOING TO MAKE YOU WHEN I BECOME A FAMOUS DOCTOR, AND CAN HELP THE PEOPLE OF THE WORLD

BUT IF I'M GOING TO BECOME A DOCTOR, I'M GOING TO HAVE TO GET GOOD GRADES IN SCHOOL...
AND TO GET GOOD GRADES, I'M GOING TO HAVE TO STUDY, AND IN ORDER TO STUDY, I HAVE TO BE HEALTHY...
IN ORDER TO BE HEALTH
I HAVE TO EAT...SO INSTEA
OF THE COLOGNE, I BOUGH
THE SANDWICH...ALL FO
YOUR HAPPINESS!

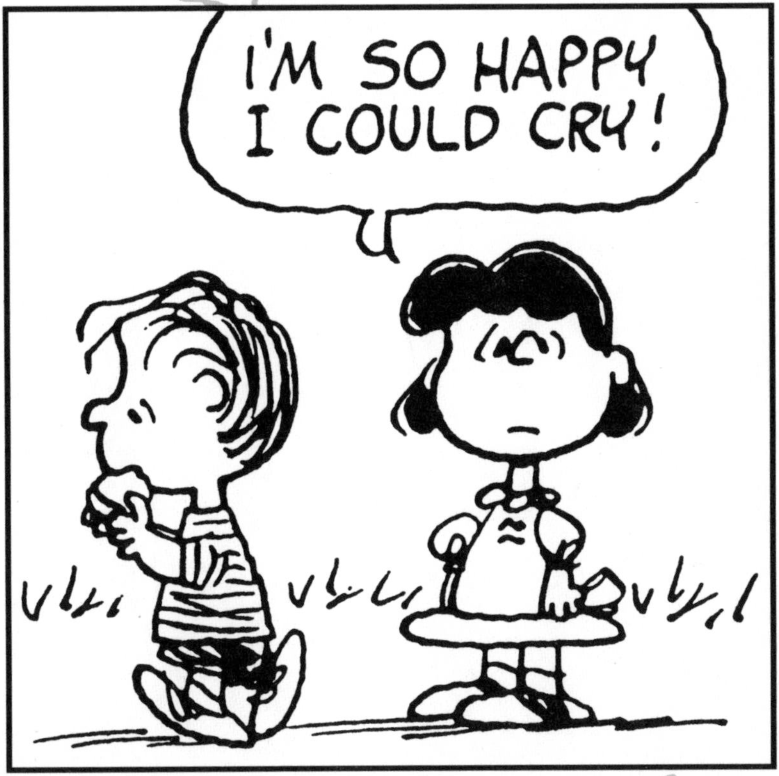
I'M SO HAPPY I COULD CRY!

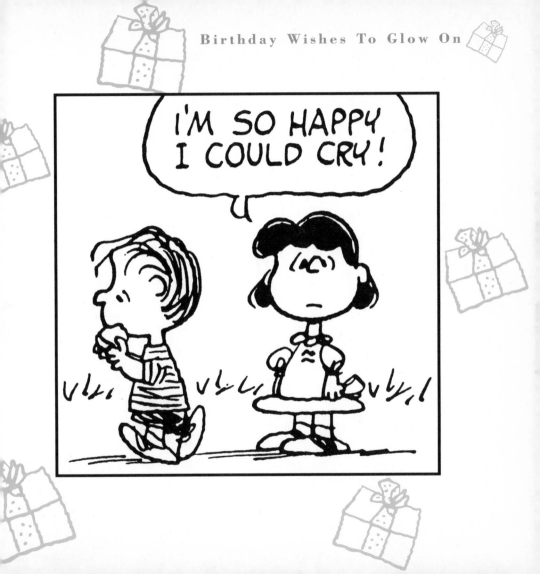

Getting On With Getting Old

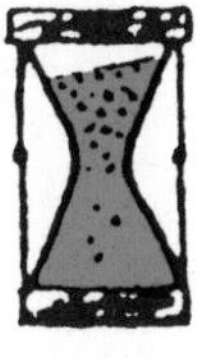

MY GRANDFATHER HAS A BIRTHDAY THIS WEEK
DOES HE MIND GETTING OLD ?
NO, HE SAYS IT DOESN'T BOTHER HIM ... IN FACT, HE SAYS HE FEELS GREAT...

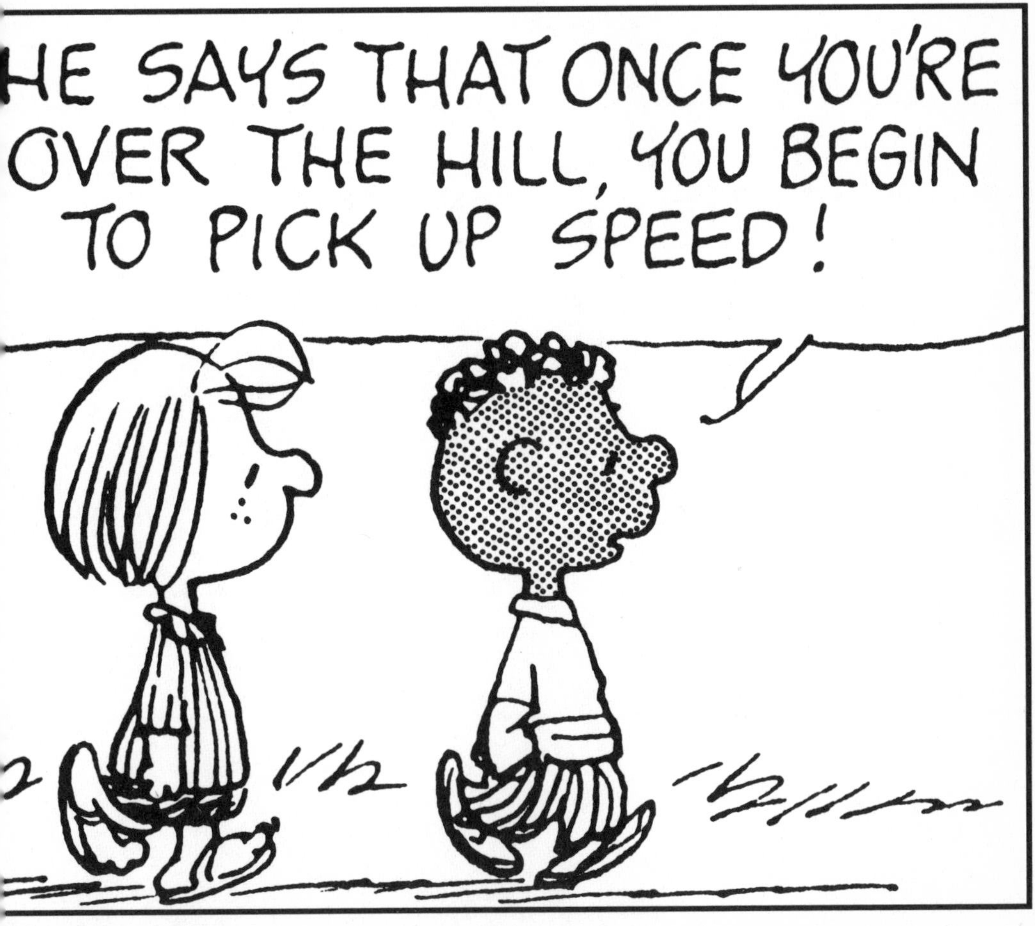
HE SAYS THAT ONCE YOU'RE OVER THE HILL, YOU BEGIN TO PICK UP SPEED!

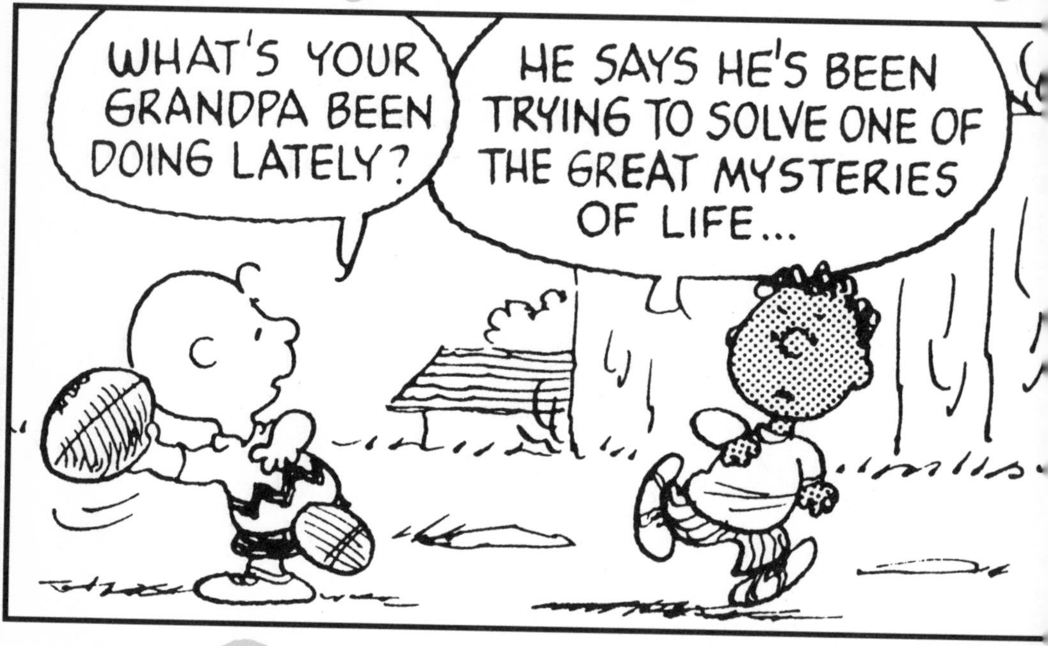
WHAT'S YOUR GRANDPA BEEN DOING LATELY?
HE SAYS HE'S BEEN TRYING TO SOLVE ONE OF THE GREAT MYSTERIES OF LIFE...

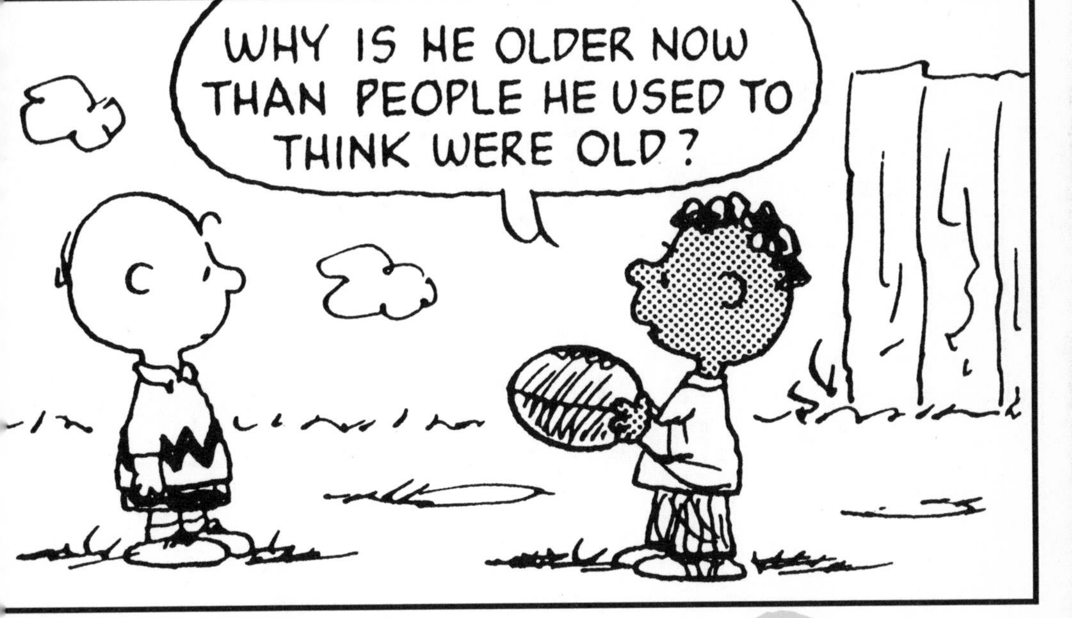
WHY IS HE OLDER NOW THAN PEOPLE HE USED TO THINK WERE OLD?

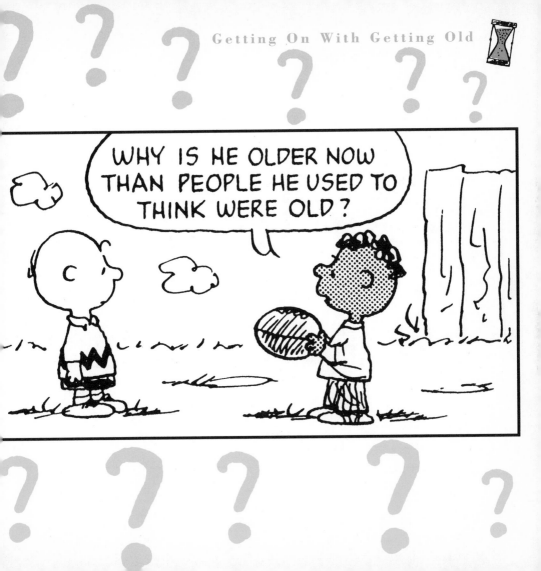

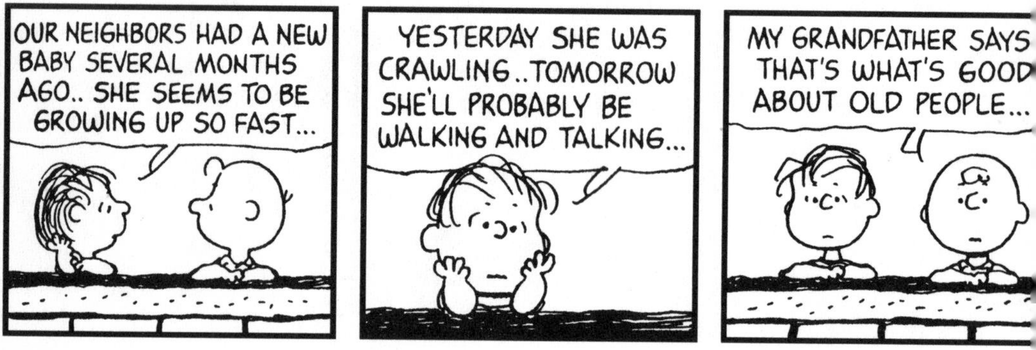
OUR NEIGHBORS HAD A NEW BABY SEVERAL MONTHS AGO.. SHE SEEMS TO BE GROWING UP SO FAST...
YESTERDAY SHE WAS CRAWLING..TOMORROW SHE'LL PROBABLY BE WALKING AND TALKING...
MY GRANDFATHER SAYS THAT'S WHAT'S GOOD ABOUT OLD PEOPLE...

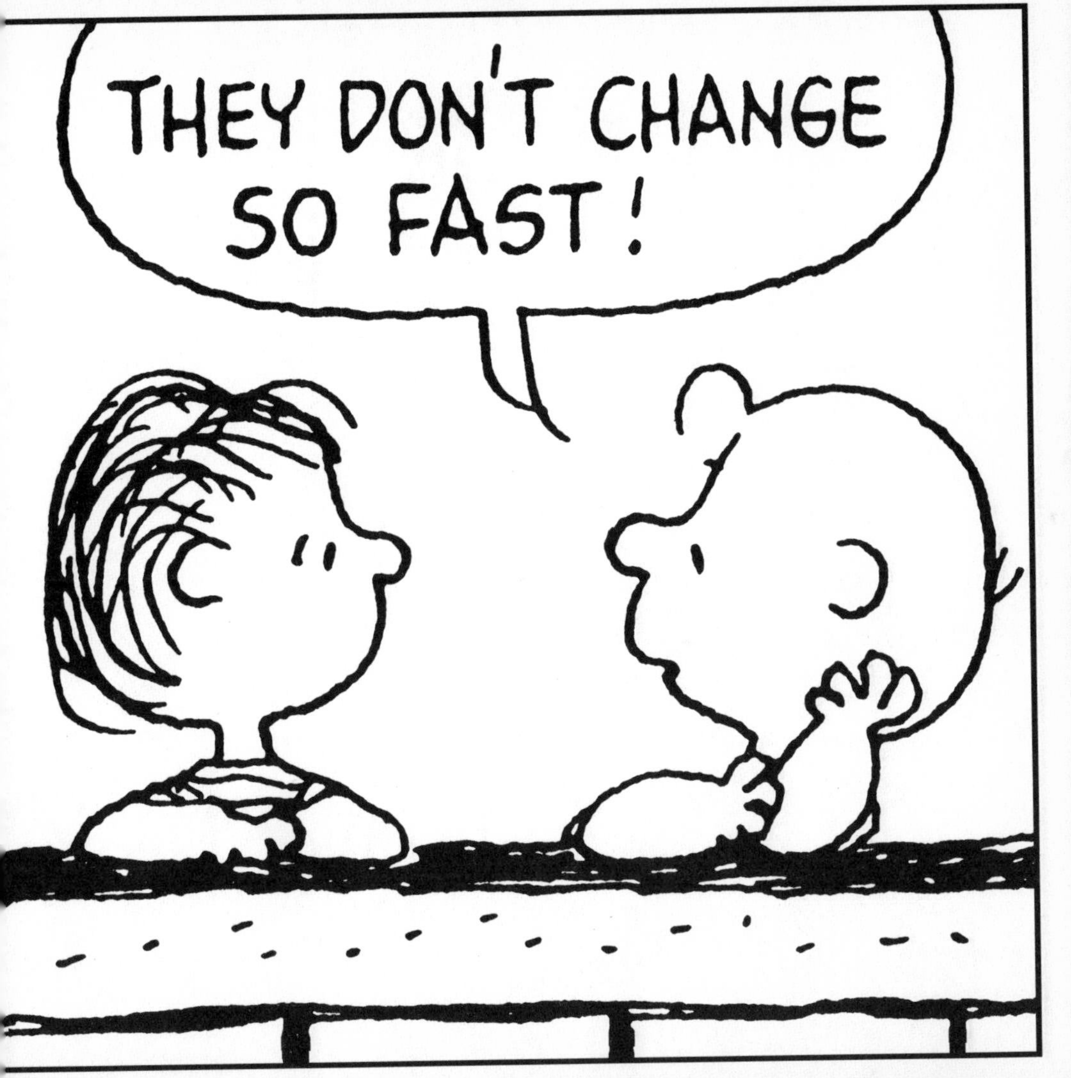
THEY DON'T CHANGE SO FAST!

A Packaged Goods Incorporated Book
First published 1996 by Collins Publishers San Francisco
1160 Battery Street, San Francisco, CA 94111-1213
http://www.harpercollins.com
Conceived and produced by Packaged Goods Incorporated
276 Fifth Avenue, New York, NY 10001
A Quarto Company

Copyright ©1996 United Feature Syndicate, Inc. All rights reserved.
HarperCollins ®, ▄®, and CollinsPublishersSanFrancisco™ are trademarks of
HarperCollins Publishers Inc.
PEANUTS is a registered trademark of United Feature Syndicate, Inc.
PEANUTS © United Feature Syndicate, Inc.
Based on the PEANUTS ® comic strip by Charles M. Schulz
http://www.unitedmedia.com

Library of Congress Cataloging-in-Publication Data
Schulz, Charles M.
[Peanuts. Selections]
Happy birthday (and one to glow on) / by Schulz.
p.   cm.
"A Packaged Goods Incorporated Book"—T.p. verso
ISBN 0-00-225039-X
I. Title
PN6728.P4S3116   1996
741.5'973—dc20   96-15195
CIP

Printed in Hong Kong

1 3 5 7 9 10 8 6 4 2

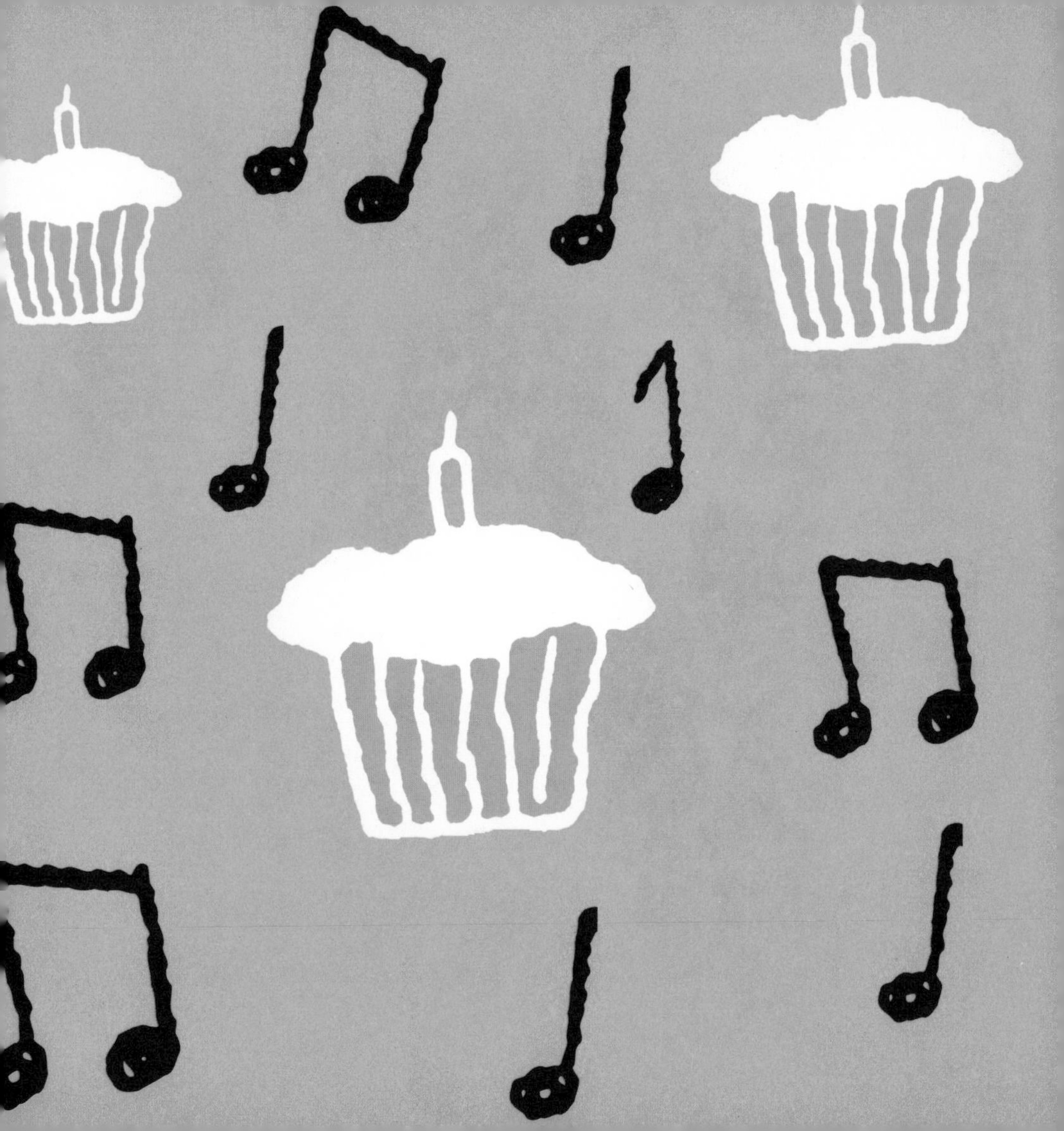

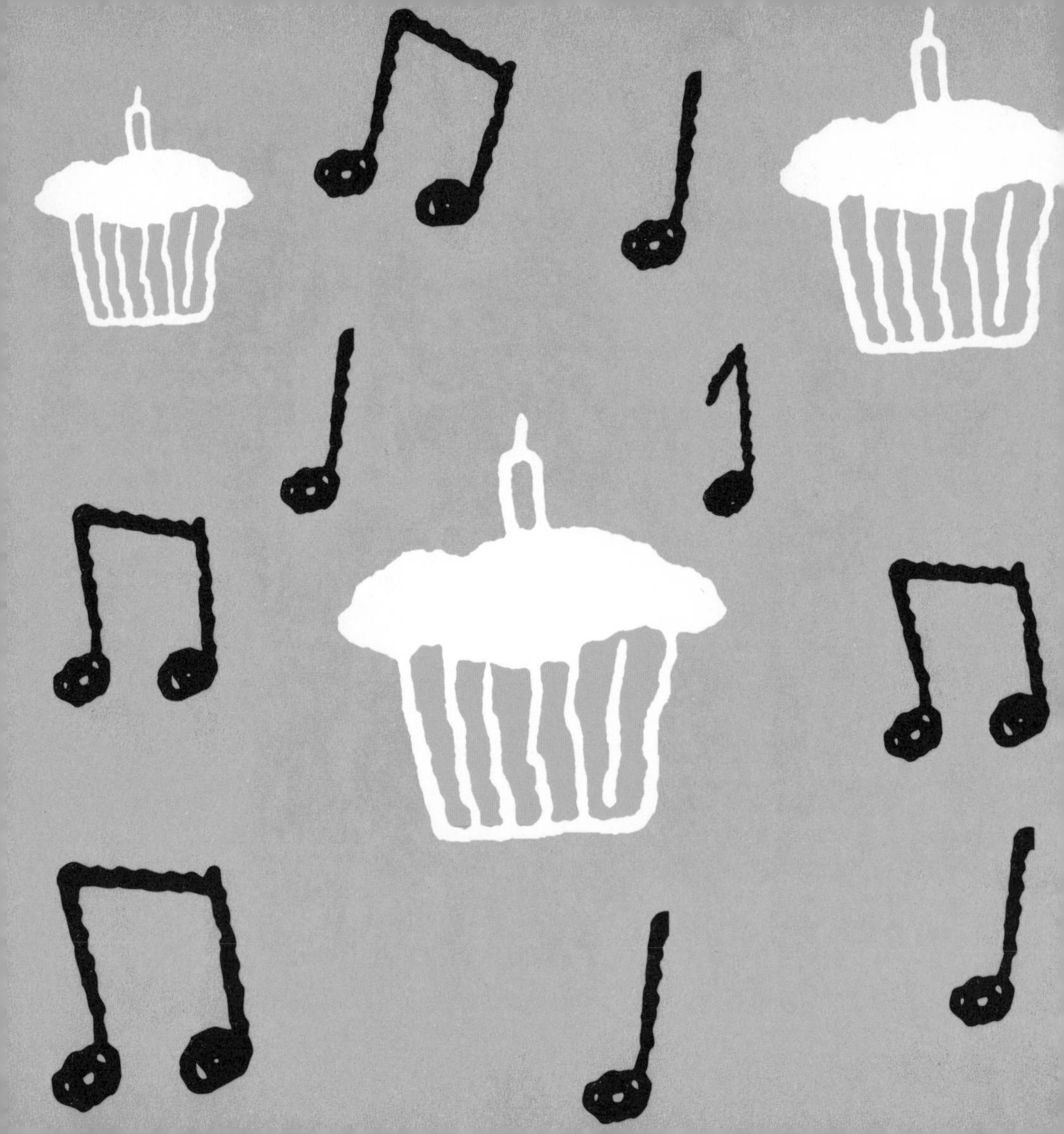